Memory

I have no room to judge, but I have plenty of room to share the truth about God's love.

Mark S. Allen

INTRODUCTION

My purpose for writing this book is to remind people that God loves them but He hates sin.

God says in His Word that it is not His will for anyone to perish but He wants everyone to repent, which means to turn away from sin. So, I began to understand why God wants people to know the truth about sin based on what He says in the Holy Bible.

I believe as the Bible teaches us that the truth will make us free from the life of sin and spiritual death. You should read the Bible for yourself and search the Scriptures that I have included in the book. I am using many Scriptures so that you will know exactly what God says about a particular subject.

A lot of pastors will not talk about the topics that I cover in this book, which will touch on the things we see daily and ignore. The book deals with the reality of what sin is, what God says about sin, and the need to be conscious of what we do and who we are as God's people.

The Bible says in Proverbs 3:5, "lean not on your own understanding" but come to the knowledge of the truth. This book can only help those who want to know the truth. I am not trying to impose my opinion on anyone. I would just ask that you allow yourself to read this with an open mind because it is meant to help you understand what the Bible says about sin.

You will find in reading this book that God's love is unconditional, but He does not have to love what we do. Remember that God loves you no matter what decision you make in life, whether you choose to know the truth about sin or whether you choose heaven or hell as your final destination. If you reject the truth about sin, there will be consequences.

I would encourage you to choose life so that you can live for eternity.

> *Now if we died with Christ, we believe that we shall also live with Him, knowing that Christ, having been raised from the dead, dies no more. Death nor longer has dominion over Him. For the death that He died, He died to sin once for all; but the life that He lives, He lives to God. Likewise you also, reckon yourselves to be dead indeed to sin, but alive to God in Christ Jesus our Lord. Therefore do not let sin reign in your mortal body, that you should obey it in its lusts. And do not present your members as instruments of unrighteousness to sin, but present yourselves to God as being alive from the dead, and your members as instruments of righteousness to God. For sin shall not have dominion over you, for you are not under law but under grace.*
>
> *—Romans 6:9-14*

CHAPTER ONE

WHAT IS SIN?

After having numerous conversations and listening to the hearts of people, I found that many of them did not understand sin and its consequences. I also discovered that some people did not know about sin because they do not read the Bible. So, I felt led to share with people what the Word of God says about sin and I used many Scriptures to support each statement. The fact is people need to know the truth which is found in Scriptures and not in man's opinion.

The Bible defines sin as turning away from God. Sin separates us from God and ultimately causes us to go to hell. This is why God hates sin because it separates us from Him in eternity. Sin can also be viewed as anything contrary to the Word of God.

There are other words that characterize sin, such as *evil*, which can be defined as a *wrong done against God*. Other definitions of *evil* includes *wickedness, immorality and malevolence,* all of which falls under the category of sin.

Whosoever committeth sin transgresseth also the law: for sin is the transgression of the law.

(1 John 3:4)

For the wages of sin is death; but the gift of God is eternal life through Jesus Christ our Lord.

(Romans 6:23)

The fear of the Lord is to hate evil: pride, and arrogancy, and the evil way, and the froward mouth, do I hate.

(Proverbs 8:13)

In this passage the word *fear* means having *reverence, respect, worship, and admiration* for the Lord.

You may say, "I don't believe in God," or "I don't believe in heaven or hell." You may even say, "I don't believe in the same God you believe in." Well, okay, but that does not change God's existence or whether you will die and end up in hell. God exists whether you believe Him or not. There is only one God. Heaven and hell exists whether you believe it or not.

There is one thing that is for sure: We all will die and spend eternity in either heaven or hell.

You may say, "You can't prove that," and you are absolutely right. So then my question becomes: "Can you prove that it is not true?" You may ask me: "Why do you believe what you believe?" I'm glad you asked me that question. I believe what I believe by faith. I also believe what I believe because of the teachings of the Word of God and the revelations I received by the Spirit of God. We have been given the choice to choose between heaven and hell, right and wrong, and good and evil. We also know there is a right way and a wrong way to live according to the knowledge we have and the Word of God.

God's Word says, "I put before you life and death..." but God then suggests to us to choose life. We read in Deuteronomy 30:19:

> *I call heaven and earth to record this day against you, that I have set before you life and death, blessing and cursing: therefore choose life, that both thou and thy seed may live.*

The Word says that "you and your seed" should live. So, that means God wants us to live.

CHAPTER TWO

WHERE WILL YOU SPEND ETERNITY?

If you died today, where would you spend eternity? Ponder that question for a moment.

What is eternity? Eternity means forever, a time that has no beginning and never ends. The dictionary defines *eternity* as *an endless state after death*. Does eternity actually exist? Some people say eternity does not exist. Some question whether there is a heaven and a hell. Does it matter?

To answer the question, we must turn to the Bible. There are two endless places, one is called *heaven* and the other is called *hell*. Did you know that *heaven* is mentioned at least 500 times in the Bible and *hell* is mentioned 54 times, according to MyBible CD and the Power BibleCD?

I believe that heaven and hell exists and it matters where we end up. Yes, it definitely matters. Everyone will spend time in one of these two places by his or her own decisions and not by

God putting you there. You will end up in heaven or hell by the choices that you make here on Earth.

If heaven is our destination after death, then we must follow the teachings of God from the Holy Bible. If we choose not to follow God's teachings, then hell will be our eternal destination after death. Hell is not God's will for our eternal life. Hell is the choice each individual makes when he or she rejects God's plan of salvation.

If we sin, we must turn to God and ask for His forgiveness. This does not give us the right to sin again. We should never make it a practice to do wrong. Because we are not perfect, we will make mistakes but that's what they are *mistakes*, things that are unforeseen, or not done on purpose.

If sin is doing what goes against the Word of God, then we should learn for ourselves what the Word of God says to do and apply it to our lives. If God tells us not to do something and we do it anyway, that is sin. Thank God that the Bible teaches us that God is merciful and will forgive us if we ask Him.

If we confess our sins, he is faithful and just to forgive us our sins and to cleanse us from all unrighteousness.

(1 John 1:9)

What does it mean to repent?

You must repent before God will forgive your sin. To *repent* means to *turn away from that which is wrong.* You can't continue to sin and think that God will forgive you for what you are still doing. You must repent!

Our judicial system is not perfect and that is why there are times when a person who actually committed a crime is set free for lack of evidence. This will never happen with God's system of justice. God is all-knowing and when we do wrong, He knows exactly what we have done. If we repent, God will forgive us. But, if we continue to do wrong, how can Jesus, as a mediator, plead our case before God if we are not willing to repent?

We were all born in sin and therefore, we are all sinners until we are saved by God's grace. The Bible says in 1 John 1:10, "If we say that we have not sinned, we make him a liar, and his word is not in us."

Grace is the deliverance we received when we accepted Jesus Christ as our Lord and Savior for His death on the cross and resurrection from death for our sins. Jesus is considered our *advocate* with the Father, according to 1 John 2:1-3 which says:

> *My little children, these things write I unto you, that ye sin not. And if any man sin, we have an advocate with the Father, Jesus Christ the righteous: And he is the propitiation for our sins: and not for ours only, but also for the sins of the whole world. And hereby we do know that we know him, if we keep his commandments.*

Right is still right and wrong is still wrong today. Times may change, but God and His Word will never change.

> *For I am the Lord, I change not; therefore ye sons of Jacob are not consumed.*

> *(Malachi 3:6)*

Jesus Christ the same yesterday, and today, and forever.

(Hebrews 13:8)

The Bible clearly tells us in Romans 3:23 that "all have sinned and come short of the glory of God." This means that every human being on the earth has missed it with God; we have all committed sin, including the Virgin Mary, the mother of our Lord and Savior Jesus Christ. Why would I say that? Because there are people who feel that Mary was perfect. God's Word says there was none perfect but Jesus Christ, who is the only One who has not sinned (Hebrews 4:14-15).

Since Jesus is the only One without sin, this means that Mary was not perfect. This is not to insult those who believe that Mary was perfect. The Scripture says Mary was chosen by God to bring the Messiah, Jesus, into the world because she was a righteous woman. She was righteous, but not perfect. God knows we are not perfect, yet He can still use whomever He wants to do His will. If you are willing and obedient God can use you, too.

There is no Scripture that proves there was anyone else without sin. However, this does not mean that we cannot strive for perfection while we are alive in the Earth. We should live a Christ-like life every day as though we are heaven-bound. The Word says it shall be "done in earth as it is in heaven." This means we should live our life as though we are in heaven, where there is no sin.

Thy kingdom come. Thy will be done in earth, as it is in heaven.

(Matthew 6:10)

So again, I ask the question: "Does eternity exist?" If by way of example we say that heaven and hell do not exist, then there is a possibility that God may not exist. And, if God does not exist, then we could do whatever we want without any consequences, except the consequences of getting caught by the law. Oops! Would there be laws if there was no God? If so, where would the laws come from? Who would create these laws and why? This is the next topic that we will explore.

The righteous shall inherit the land, and dwell therein forever. The mouth of the righteous speaketh wisdom, and his tongue talketh of judgment. The law of his God is in his heart; none of his steps shall slide. The wicked watcheth the righteous, and seeketh to slay him. The Lord will not leave him in his hand, nor condemn him when he is judged. Wait on the Lord, and keep his way, and he shall exalt thee to inherit the land: when the wicked are cut off, thou shall see it. I have seen the wicked in great power, and spreading himself like a green bay tree. Yet he passed away, and lo, he was not: yea, I sought him, but he could not be found. Mark the perfect man, and behold the upright: for the end of that man is peace. But the transgressors shall be destroyed together: the end of the wicked shall be cut off. But the salvation of the righteous is of the Lord: he is their strength in the time of trouble. And the Lord shall help them, and deliver them: he shall deliver them from the wicked, and save them, because they trust in him.

—Psalm 37:29-40

CHAPTER 3

WHAT IF THERE WERE NO GOD AND NO LAWS?

I remember watching a movie called, "Mad Max 2: The Road Warrior," starring Mel Gibson. The setting was in a post-apocalyptic wasteland. The world had become a desolate place because "two mighty warrior tribes" had gone to war. The survivors who stayed together were starving, and water and fuel were scarce. There were also outcast, hard-core criminals who harassed the survivors, who had no peace or protection from them. The criminals stopped at nothing to take what they wanted. Mel Gibson's character, "Max," was an ex-cop who had lost his wife and son to these same type of criminals and was now a drifter. Max eventually helped the survivors escape from the criminals and start a new life elsewhere.

In this movie, everyone was out of control and survived the best way they could. There were no rules and there were no laws to protect the people. Movies such as this one gives us an idea of what the world would be like today without God. Can you imagine a world without laws? Can you imagine what it would be like if there was no God? If there were no God and no laws, there would be no protection for people, and truly, only the strong would survive. I would never want to live in that kind of world. We ought to be thankful that God exists and that He implemented laws to keep the world in order.

This is one of the reasons why I know that God exists: He set laws in place to keep the world in order. If the chances are, as some people believe, that God, heaven and hell are not real, or if there is a 50-50 chance that they are real, then the question you need to ask yourself is: "Am I willing to roll the dice and gamble on my life for eternity?" That's huge! Yet, this is what people are doing every day with their lives: They are willing to take a chance on whether eternity is real or not.

No one can physically prove to you that God, heaven and hell are real. But, no one can prove to you that God, heaven and hell are not real. If I'm right in my decision to believe that God is real and receive Jesus Christ as my personal Lord and Savior, I will go on to live an eternal life in the Kingdom of Heaven with God and other believers forever. But those who reject the plan of salvation will spend eternity in a place with all their greatest fears, pain and suffering and have no relief. God has made it so simple to receive salvation just by confessing, believing and receiving Jesus Christ as our personal Lord and Savior and by obeying the Word of God. Jesus said in Matthew 11:29-30, "Take my yoke upon you, and learn of me; for I am meek and lowly in heart: and ye shall find rest unto your souls. For my yoke is easy, and my burden is light."

Now of course if I am wrong and you are right, then we will all just cease to exist and there would be no judgment. If my decision to choose Jesus is wrong I have nothing to lose. But, if you decide not to choose Jesus as Lord then you have made the worst decision for your life that you will ever make, and the last.

If the case being, once you are dead, you're dead, then why fear death? Death would be the ultimate problem-solver. People who are troubled with all sorts of problems would look to death to rid themselves of their problems. Why not? If all that would happen is that you cease to exist and there is no consequence or no judgment for wrong-doing, why not? Why would you allow yourself to suffer any torment of the world and all its problems if you will just cease to exist when you die? Some people believe that they will just cease to exist, and so they make the decision to die by killing themselves.

But if you are wrong about God and you make the wrong decision concerning God, you will spend eternity in hell where you will suffer in torment forever. Now those who have received God's gift of salvation through Jesus Christ should not fear death because death is a transition into the next life in heaven. Earth and all of its problems does not compare to hell, also called, "the fiery furnace." Some people may tell you, "That's not true, there is no hell." They may even say, "What kind of God would create us just so He could torment us later for not doing what He said?" No, God did not create you just to torment you later. You did this because of the decision you made in not making Jesus Christ as your Lord and Savior.

Remember, God's Word tells us that God put before us life and death, blessings and cursings, heaven and hell; so, the choice is ours.

God is Love

God is a loving God. He loves us unconditionally with the *agape* kind of love. *Agape* is a Greek word that means *love*. It's the kind of love that says, "I love you whether you love me or not." We should love God, too. We do that by following Him and being obedient to His Word. The Bible is our guide and gives us instructions on how we ought to live and love God. Great men have fallen in our history because they rejected this awesome plan that God set in place for His creation.

God loves people, God loves His creation, and God loves His children. Because of God's love for us, He sent His son, Jesus, to die for the sins of the world.

> *For God so loved the world, that he gave his only begotten Son, that whosoever believeth in him (***who? Jesus, that's who***) should not perish, but have everlasting life. For God sent not his Son into the world to condemn the world; but that the world through him (***who? Jesus, that's who***) might be saved. He that believeth on him is not condemned: but he that believeth not is condemned already, because he hath not believed in the name (***authority of Jesus***) of the only begotten Son of God* (John 3:16- 18, words in parentheses added for emphasis).

Because God loves us, He also tells us to love one another. Love, then, is the true spirit of God. We should put God first by choosing Jesus as our personal Lord and Savior and applying the Word of God to our lives.

You see, the problem is not that God doesn't love you or want you, the problem lies with you rejecting God. If you reject God, that means you do not love God. The Bible says in 1 John 4:8, "He that loveth not knoweth not God; for God is Love." God set certain things in place that He will not change till the earth has run its course. Two of those things are life and death. So, where you choose to spend eternity is your choice, not God's. When you read the Word of God, you will see that it is not God's will that any should perish. Hell was never meant for man. Hell was not made for God's people, but for satan and the angels who disobeyed God and followed satan. If they were judged because they disobeyed God, then how are we to escape the wrath of God?

For if God spared not the angels that sinned, but cast them down to hell, and delivered them into chains of darkness, to be reserved unto judgment; And spared not the old world, but saved Noah the eighth person, a preacher of righteousness, bringing in the flood upon the world of the ungodly; And turning the cities of Sodom and Gomorrha into ashes condemned them with an overthrow, making them an ensample unto those that after should live ungodly; And delivered just Lot, vexed with the filthy conversation of the wicked: For that righteous man dwelling among them, in seeing and hearing, vexed his righteous soul from day to day with their unlawful deeds; The Lord knoweth how to deliver the godly out or temptations, and to reserve the unjust unto the day of judgment to be punished.

(2 Peter 2:4-9)

Don't let people fool you by telling you there is no hell or there is no punishment for doing wrong. Trust God's word, not man's opinion. We read in Romans 3:4, "God forbid: ye, let God be true, but every man a liar, as it is written, That thou mightest be justified in thy sayings, and mightest overcome when thou art judged." The Bible also teaches us in Deuteronomy 4:2 not to add or take away from the Word of God, "that ye may keep the commandments of the Lord your God..."

Jesus is the only way to God

There is only one way to the Father and it is through Jesus Christ, His Son. You may ask, "How can you say that Jesus is the only way to God the Father and the only way to enter the Kingdom of God?" Jesus Himself said it in John 14:6, "I am the way, the truth and the life: no man cometh unto the Father, but by me." *I* didn't say it, *Jesus* said it. I received it and I am acting on that which I believe is truth. I believe the Bible whether I can prove it or not. It's called *faith*. Faith doesn't say, "Prove it." Faith says, "Only believe."

There are many, many religions in the world today and they have no proof of their god but, they believe that their god is real. All these religions have great promises of eternal life of some sort, right? But how can they be sure? The Bible teaches believers that signs shall follow those that believe on His name and by faith, we can be confident of this by the Word of God. If you are a believer, signs are following you. The Bible also testifies of many things that have happened. The Bible shares with us a beginning and what will happen in the end. The Bible has already proven itself to be the truth by many events that have occurred and those things that were prophesied to happen.

When we deny that Jesus is the Christ, the Son of the Living God, then we are rejecting God. The Bible teaches that Jesus is One with the Father:

> *For there are three that bear record in heaven, the Father, the Word, and the Holy Ghost: and these three are one. And there are three that bear witness in earth, the Spirit, and the water, and the blood: and these three agree in one. If we receive the witness of men, the witness of God is greater: for this is the witness of God which he hath testified of his Son. He that believeth on the Son of God hath the witness in himself: he that believeth not God hath made him a liar; because he believeth not the record that God gave of his Son. And this is the record, that God hath given to us eternal life, and this life is in his Son.*
>
> *(1 John 5:7-11)*

Any Bible that does not say this, throw it away! It is our responsibility to know if there is a God and the truth about God. Hey, listen, neither your momma nor your daddy can help you here. This is something you had better be absolutely sure of; this is a decision for *you* and *you alone.* I declare that we should all take a good look at ourselves and be sure of where we want to end up for eternity. Eternity is forever. Do you know where you will spend eternity? Don't guess, be sure! No one can make this decision for you. Do you know your death date? What if you don't wake up? Every night we assume or expect to see another day. Maybe we are taking life for granted. Do you think we are promised to see another day? This is why we must make the right decision now while we are living. Once we die, judgment is final. There is no probation, there is no getting out on good behavior, and there is no purgatory.

For centuries, man has tried to play God by believing that he can rule the world. Man would like for you to think that God did not create the world, it just fell into existence. This is one of the most ridiculous things that man could come up with!

This is something man came up with so that he would not have any one to answer to for his sins and wrong-doings!

People who have chosen to believe that God does not exist feel they can live their life any way they want. Many prominent people live their lives thinking they have achieved greatness but, they don't understand that without God, they don't have anything. Nothing you have achieved in this life, whether it is wealth or power, can gain you a place in heaven with God. The one thing God cares about is people. If you have not put God first in your life by serving Him, then your wealth is nothing. No one has taken their wealth or power with them into the next life. Matthew 16:26 asks the question: "For what is a man profited, if he shall gain the whole world, and lose his own soul? or what shall a man give in exchange for his soul?"

There is nothing wrong with being rich except when you allow the riches to control you. When that happens, you will do anything to get it and anything to keep it. There are some things you just cannot buy no matter how much money you have. No one can buy more years to add to his or her life. No one can buy back health, or youth, or the times you lost with love ones. Most of all, *no one can buy God.*

We need to take a closer look at our lives because a person who doesn't think they need God is making a decision to reject God. Remember, this is a free-will decision to make and neither you nor I can stop a person's free-will decision.

God Himself won't interfere with your free-will decision. God will try to help us to make a godly decision by his Spirit. But our free will gives us the choice to choose or reject God. God wants us to freely choose Him as He has chosen us. Salvation is open to everyone. The choice to receive it is up to you.

> *Let not sin therefore reign in your mortal body, that ye should obey it in the lusts thereof. Neither yield ye your members as instruments of unrighteousness unto sin: but yield yourselves unto God, as those that are alive from the dead, and your members as instruments of righteousness unto God. For sin shall not have dominion over you: for ye are not under the law, but under grace. What then? shall we sin because we are not under the law, but under grace? God forbid. Know ye not, that to whom ye yield yourselves servants to obey, his servants ye are to whom ye obey; whether of sin unto death, or of obedience unto righteousness? But God be thanked, that ye were the servants of sin, but ye have obeyed from the heart that form of doctirne which was delivered you. Being then made free from sin, ye became the servants of righteousness…For the wages of sin is death; but the gift of God is eternal life through Jesus Christ our Lord.*
>
> *–Romans 6:12-18,23*

CHAPTER 4

WHO ARE THE UNRIGHTEOUS?

Just as the Bible speaks about those who believe in God, it also speaks plainly about those who reject God. The Bible calls those who reject God *unrighteous.*

The unrighteous are people who disobey God's laws, worship false gods, and live a sinful lifestyle that prevents them from entering into the Kingdom of Heaven.

We read in the Word of God about men being "lovers of themselves." We can see all of this today. People boast about themselves without giving glory to God for what they have accomplished. They are also unthankful and unholy and have no conviction about the sins they commit or how they treat others. Simply put, the unrighteous are people who will go to hell if they do not repent.

You might ask, "What sins could they possibly commit that would send them to hell if they do not repent?" The Bible lists a few of them in 1 Corinthians 6:9-10:

> *Know ye not that the unrighteous shall not inherit the kingdom of God? Be not deceived: neither fornicators, nor idolaters, nor adulterers, nor effeminate, nor abusers of themselves with mankind, nor thieves, nor covetous, nor drunkards, nor revilers, nor extortioners, shall inherit the kingdom of God.*

Let's take a closer look at each of these sins.

Fornicators

Who are fornicators? Fornicators are unmarried men or women who have sex out of wedlock. God says this is the only sin where humans sin against themselves. For example, it is a sin for men and women who are not married to live together like husband and wife, defiling themselves. Although they may ask for forgiveness, if they continue to commit fornication, then they have not repented at all. You can say, "The Lord forgives me" but He does not forgive you if you refuse to turn away from sin. The one thing we should keep in mind is that God is all-knowing and all-seeing. So, if your prayer is not sincere, then God will know it. You can't fool God.

The entertainment industry is probably one of the biggest reasons we are falling into sinful lifestyles today. The industry tells us how to talk, how to walk, how to dress, how to think, what to eat and what to drink, what is acceptable and what is not acceptable. Hollywood promotes this behavior because entertainers do whatever feels good to them. But, just because something feels good does not mean that it is good for you.

It feels good to have a person in your life that you deeply love, but if you discover that the feelings are not mutual, it can be devastating. I know sex feels good but if you are not married and you have sex, it is sin. You won't feel so great when you find out that you contracted a life-threatening sexually transmitted disease or when you discover you're pregnant after having casual sex. You also won't feel so great if you die without repenting for your sin and have to stand before God to explain that your fifteen minutes of sexual pleasure meant more to you than God's Son suffering for you on the Cross. And, it's all because you were using for fun what God proclaimed as holy. Don't be fooled by what looks good or what feels good.

Forsaking fornication and following God's way, which is marriage, is essential for living a blessed life. God ordained marriage between a man and a woman from the very beginning. Marriage is a God-ordained, legal agreement between a man and woman joined together in holy matrimony. God's purpose for marriage is for men and women to reproduce to replenish the earth and to fulfill the desires of one another as *husband* and *wife*.

Keep in mind that it is called holy matrimony because God is involved. God is the One who joins, or spiritually connects man and woman together, as He did Adam and Eve. Marriage originated with Adam and Eve. That is why in order for us to understand marriage and its purpose, we need to look in the Bible. Marriage was never man's idea. We know

Memory

by Theodore Sturgeon

that men would not come up with anything that would limit the number of women they could have in their lives! Marriage was not designed by the Church or by religion, but by God.

And (Jesus) said, For this cause shall a man leave father and mother, and shall cleave to his wife: and they twain shall be one flesh? Wherefore they are no more twain, but one flesh. What therefore God hath joined together, let not man put asunder.

(Matthew 19:5-6)

Therefore shall a man leave his father and his mother, and shall cleave unto his wife: and they shall be one flesh.

(Genesis 2:24)

Marriage is honourable in all, and the bed undefiled: but whoremongers and adulterers God will judge.

(Hebrews 13:4)

Since God created marriage, what authority does anyone have to alter what comes from Him? Sex should only be between a *husband* and his *wife*. Why? Because God said it and that should be good enough! In addition, sex outside of marriage has an effect on the family and causes hurt when people take advantage of one another. Sex is not just two people reaching a climax, but it is an inward feeling of the heart of married people expressing their love for one another. If you are not married and you are having sex, you are not in love, but in lust. Real love will not gamble on one's eternal life.

The Word says in 1 Corinthians 7:9 that "it's better to marry than to burn," this means that people who have sex without being married will go to hell when they die. This also means that if we cannot control our sexual desires, then we should get married rather than burn in hell for being fornicators. Knowing what I know today, I would not want to put myself or anyone else in the position to be judged by God. I'm not throwing any stones at any one because I once lived this life of sin in committing fornication with women I dated. I once heard a person say, "Why don't you make that woman a righteous woman?" This was not a comment directed toward me, but it captured my attention. I was curious about what the statement meant. At the time, I was living a fornicated lifestyle with my girlfriend who would soon become my wife. Reading the Bible and hearing the Word taught on the subject by Dr. Fred K.C. Price, helped me to understand that righteousness meant living the life God says to live. I made a choice to change the way I was living. I loved my girlfriend, but I loved God even more! So, that settled it for me! Marriage was the way for me. I believe we would have continued to live in sin had one of us not heard the Word of God on the subject of fornication. My wife and I have been married since 1991. This is God's grace!

The Bible says to "flee fornication." The word *flee* means *to run, to get away, to separate yourself* as quickly as possible from the very temptation that would separate you from God. Sin separates us from God. First Corinthians 6:18 says, "Flee fornication. Every sin that a man doeth is without the body; but he that committeth fornication sinneth against his own body."

Adultery

People who are married and cheat on their spouse have committed adultery. Unless they repent, they will not inherit the Kingdom of God. When people commit adultery, they are not just cheating on their spouses, they are cheating in the face of God. They are dishonoring and breaking a sworn oath that they made before God.

Wedding vows are a sworn oath between two people to be faithful and committed to one another "till death do your part." In other words, death is one of the things that separates a husband and a wife. We also recognize divorce as another thing that separates us from our spouses, though we read in the Bible that this was not God's original design for us to ever go through a divorce:

> *He saith unto them, Moses because of the hardness of your hearts suffered you to put away your wives: but from the beginning it was not so. And I say unto you, Whosoever shall put away his wife, except it be for fornication, and shall marry another, committeth adultery: and whoso marrieth her which is put away doth commit adultery.*

> *(Matthew 19:8-9)*

> *But whoso committeth adultery with a woman lacketh under- standing: he that doeth it destroyeth his own soul.*

> *(Proverbs 6: 32)*

Adultery destroys marriages which, in many cases, end in divorce. This is not God's original design for marriage. It is too bad that some people do not respect marriage the way God intended for it to be respected.

Idolaters

The Bible says idolaters will not enter into the Kingdom of God. Who are idolaters? Idolaters are people who worship idols or believe in a god that is different from the God of the Bible. The Bible shares many stories of people who believe in and worship false gods.

We should love the Lord our God with all of our heart, soul, mind, and with all our strength. The Bible teaches that God is the Only True and Living God and He does not want us to worship or serve any other god.

> *Thou shalt have no other gods before me. Thou shalt not make unto thee any graven image, or any likeness of any thing that is in heaven above, or that is in the earth beneath, or that is in the water under the earth: Thou shalt not bow down thyself to them, nor serve them: for I the Lord thy God am a jealous God.*
>
> *(Exodus 20:3-5)*

Now, God is not like man in that He is insecure and lacks confidence to hold on to what belongs to Him. The word *jealous* in the Bible is defined as taking God's glory and giving it to someone or something else. The Israelites did this in the Bible:

And he received them at their hand, and fashioned it with a graving tool, after he had made it a molten calf: and they said, These be thy gods, O Israel which brought thee up out of the land of Egypt.

(Exodus 32:4)

Israel made their own gods with their own hands and worshiped them. They gave the glory of God to other gods and idols. What have you made your god?

Sometimes we allow things, and even people, to have precedence in our lives, thereby separating us from God. Not keeping God first can only mean that something or someone else is taking priority in your life. God's command is that He be first in our life. Anything that you can't do without, you are making it a priority in your life. This has become your idol. People tend to put other people or things before God, forgetting that it is God who gives us life.

Some people are even willing to kill themselves because they have allowed people, or the pressures of life, to mean more to them than God. They don't understand God's love. God sent His Son to die for the sins of the world. A high ransom has been paid for us because of sin. Therefore, we should not allow anything to come before God. This grieves the Spirit of God or should we say, it makes him angry. We should never give God's glory to any person or thing. So, remove your idols and follow God. God considers you a great price or He would not have given the best ransom for you.

Again, the kingdom of heaven is like unto a merchant man, seeking goodly pearls: Who, when he had found one pearl of great price, went and sold all that he had, and bought it.

(Matthew 13:45-46)

God gave His Son, Jesus, for you. How many of you are prepared to give your child for the world to be saved?

Thieves

The Bible teaches us that thieves, people who take from others, will not enter into the Kingdom of God, according to 1 Corinthians 6:10. Stealing causes hurt and loss to others, and in most cases, those who have had things stolen from them are unable to replace that which was lost.

People who steal are heartless and have no consideration or respect for others or their property. The price they will pay is never going to be worth what they have taken. First Peter 4:15 says, "For let none of you suffer as a murderer, or a thief, or an evil-doer, or as a meddler in other men's matters." It does not matter whether you are a murderer, a thief, or a meddler in other men's matters, those who partake in these sins will be judged. You can see from this Scripture that a thief is compared to a murderer.

Revilers

Revilers are people who speak with contemptuous, abusive, disgraceful or shameful language. To speak abusively means to have a foul mouth, as when one curses.

Jeremy Jedd stood in the igneous dust of the spaceport margin, staring into the sky and shading his eyes with his arm. Occasionally he checked the time by his ristkron, shaking it to make sure it was wound, craning back toward the hunched Customs House and the great clock. The sign there announced placidly that the *Pinnacle* had reported, was overdue, and would discharge passengers at Gate Three.

Jeremy shook his head and took the letter from Mars out of his pocket again. Slowly he unfolded it and read, in the manner of a man checking his mnemonics. He was certainly familiar enough with it, after so much re-reading. The letter said:

You must have heard by this time that General Export has installed a fabricating plant here, just outside Fort Wargod. It cost them plenty in time and money to get it set up—actually most of it was shipped as hand luggage because of the shipping space situation.

Like a lot of other people, I thought it was a foolish move, because the finished piping they could have shipped in the space is at such a premium on Mars, and because their plant is going to require power—a hard thing to get here. I didn't worry too much, though. Why should we care what our competitors do with their money?

But here's the joker. In spite of the fact that the plant is small and comparatively crude, it will fabricate pipe. And the material is plastic, chum, and they can now ship it in sheets! I don't have to tell you what that means to us. We only got our cargo-space contracts from General Export because the Government okayed our shipping system—nesting the smaller diameters of pipe inside the larger ones. Genex's own pipe is shipped that way now, too. The idea isn't patentable.

So unless we find a patentable way to ship pipe in less space, finished, than Genex is taking for their sheet-stock, we're done, brother—wiped out. Genex means to get everything in the Colonial System—you know that. They have all the ships now, and most of the goods and services. I'm afraid we're going on the long list of small operators who have tried to buck them.

Jeremy lowered the letter and rubbed his eyes again. They ached. Since he had received it a week ago, he hadn't slept much. Supplying pipe for the Mars project was work enough without these long nights in the laboratory trying to figure a way out of this spot. Everything he and Hal had in the world was in this deal. They had worked together ever since they left school, right up until the time Hal went up to handle the Mars end.

Fervently he wished it were the other way around. If Hal were here, he'd dope out something. He had always been the real brains of Jedd & Jedd. And as a matter of

Memory

fact, Hal already had doped out something. What an irony! Whatever his process or system was, he couldn't write it or wire it. General Export carried the mails too, and if they wanted to find something out, it would be only too easy.

*

Jeremy looked up again. There was a growing, gleaming dot in the sky. He glanced at the building. Near it, men were manning the heatproof launch. He turned back to the letter, to read the cryptic part about Phyllis Exeter:

I know a way to whip this, bud. I'm not telling you about it in a letter—you know why. I'm hoping and praying that you'll figure it out yourself. The new hauling contracts are coming up, and priorities for shipping space go to the pipe company that can pack the most in. My process is very simple, really. It's nothing that Budgie couldn't have told you. You have three weeks to figure it out after you get this note, and don't forget it takes ten days to file a patent application.

And in connection with this idea, Phyllis Exeter is due to arrive on the *Pinnacle*. I'd like you to meet her when the rocket-ship docks. She really has what it takes. I got quite chummy with her while she was out here in Thor City. She'll probably have a lot to say about it. She'll have a lot to say, period. She talks more than Budgie. Be good, little man.

Jeremy's brows matted together as he folded the note and put it away. There was more than met the eye in those last two paragraphs—much more. He got some of it. "Be good, little man." And the references to Budgie—he wasn't too sure, but he had the idea they weren't in there for the purpose of using up ink. And the specific mention of Phyllis Exeter and her arrival. Now, *that* was something.

If Hal wanted to be absolutely positive Phyllis Exeter would see him, he'd sure picked the right way. Just that line in the letter would be enough to have Phyllis hunt him up anywhere on Earth, even if he hid. General Export carried the mails. But why Phyllis? After all, Hal and Phyllis had been—He shrugged. If Hal wanted to throw them together again, all right. He began to get the old, familiar feeling, just thinking about it.

From overhead came the blow-torch susurrus of the *Pinnacle's* braking and hovering jets. Down she came on her bed of fire, until she hesitated at five thousand feet. He distinctly heard the sudden shift to cold-jets, and in another minute the dust-cloud was piled up to receive her.

Jeremy stepped into the waiting room of Number Three Gate, just avoiding the sudden angry gusts of dust-laden air. He shouldered past the chattering crowd

6

What people say, *and how they say it,* is important to God. The Bible says that men will give an account for every idle word that comes out of their mouths. Jesus said in Matthew 12:36, "But I say unto you, that every idle word that men shall speak, they shall give account thereof in the day of judgment."

Don't fool yourself; having a foul mouth is sin, too. It is an abusive language and it affects your behavior. First Corinthians 15:33 says, "Be not deceived; evil communications corrupt good manners." You may be thinking, "Aw, man, come on! Some people do this all the time and they make people laugh." You are right, but the Bible says we shall give an account for every word that comes out of our mouth. If the language is foul it is sin. This is not limited to cursing; what you say *about* people and how you say things *to* people are very important to God as well. The Bible warns us in Galatians 6:7: "Be not deceived; God is not mocked: for whatsoever a man soweth, that shall he also reap."

Gamblers

Gambling is not found in 1 Corinthians 6:9-10 but I wanted to add this to show you the chances people are willing to take with their lives in the earth and for eternity.

Don't gamble with eternity for your life. Besides gambling is wrong. WHAT? Yeah, it's wrong. How can you say that? Did you know that God also tells us He would give us the desires of our heart? God teaches us to lay our cares on Him. God says in His Word that He would supply all of our needs according to His riches in glory. So, there is no need to gamble with life or your finances when God supplies your needs.

But my God shall supply all your need according to his riches in glory by Christ Jesus.

(Philippians 4:19)

Casting all your care upon him; for he careth for you.

(1 Peter 5:7)

Delight thyself also in the LORD; and he shall give thee the desires of thine heart.

(Psalm 37:4)

What's wrong with gambling? Gambling is putting your hopes in chance. This also causes people to put their hopes in other people's failures. In order for you to win, someone else has to lose, and that's what gambling is all about. God does not want any of us to lose. God wants us to trust in Him, not the numbers or lottery, nor bingo or any other form of gambling.

God wants us to be winners or should we say, more than conquerors in all that He has for us. God wants the best for His children, just like you would want the best for your children.

Gambling is not of God. So, stop thanking God for lottery winnings. God is not a respecter of persons. He would not allow others to suffer so that one of His children can win the lottery. People who gamble lose more than they win. Because of that, they take on the physical stress that goes with gambling.

God is a God of faith and blessings. He wants us to be in a win-win situation. How would you feel as a parent to see your children gambling all that they had and knowing only inside and got to a port, which was covered with a disc of transparent plastic whirling at high speed to afford clear vision through the mucky dust which hurtled so violently about the building. From the spaceport central, the little heatproof drifted toward the grounding liner, waiting its chance to settle on the huge hull and sink its extensible airlock into the monster like an ovipositor.

Fifteen minutes later the heatproof whickered slowly down to the roof of the gate building. The crowd pressed toward the elevators and was shunted back by the page-boys and officials. Jeremy stood on the fringes, trying to look indifferent and doing a very poor job of it.

The first load came down. A heavy-set man with a dark, rocky face. A quick, slender, cold-eyed man. These two stood aside and let a woman with two children and an aged couple pass them. And then Phyllis stepped out.

He wondered again, looking at her, what a man would have to do to ruffle that sleekness, to crumple the brilliant mask she seemed to wear. Throw a kiss or a fist in that face, and there would be little difference. Her hair was soft, and iridescent green, now. She smoked with a long holder, and the smoke matched her hair. Her voice was as lustrous, as colorful as ever, when she saw him.

"Jeremy!" she said. "Jeremy Jedd! How are you, darling?"

"Don't call me darling," he said.

"Oh, these people won't think anything of me that they don't think already," she said.

"They might think it of me," he said grimly. He took her arm, while she laughed as if trying to find out whether she could. She could.

"Come on," he said. "I need a drink. Before, I just wanted one."

She hung back and pouted. "You seem quite sure I'll come."

"You've been reading my mail!" he quipped grimly. She stopped hanging back. They moved toward the door and down the short path to the Customs House. Jeremy glanced back. The two men he had noticed at the elevators were following them. He gestured slightly with his head. "Yours?"

She shrugged. "Oh, you know how it is."

"No," he said, "I don't. Not altogether. But I'll learn the rest of it."

*

She laughed again, and hugged his elbow close to her body. "Jeremy," she said cozily, "do you still feel the same way about me?"

He glanced down into her wide gray-green eyes. "Yup. Always will, I guess. Worse luck."

"Worse luck?"

"It gets in my hair," he grumbled. "When I think of all the time I've spent thinking about you when I could've been making pipe—"

"That's what I like about you," she flashed. "You make a person feel so welcome." She released his arm. "What makes you think you can treat me like that?"

"Several things. They all add up to the fact that you won't walk away from me until you find out what you think I know about stowing pipe. No matter what I say or do to you, you'll tag right along."

"All right," she said, in quite a new, matter-of-fact voice. "I'd just as soon play that way then. All the cards face up, and such sordidness. It could have been pleasant, too."

"Not with me. Not with you and me."

"That's what I meant."

Inside the building they turned to the right elevator bank and dropped to the cafeteria two levels below. There was no conversation in the elevator due to the silent presence of the two men who had followed them from the gatehouse. Jeremy glared at them, but the younger man refused to catch his eye and stared at the ceiling, whistling softly. The other man gazed at Phyllis's feet.

"I think," Jeremy said, as they emerged, "that you have hired these pugs just to bolster your ego. You'll have men following you whatever you have to do."

"It isn't necessary to hire them for that," she said coldly. "I'm sorry you find this unpleasant, Jeremy. But please don't make it any more so than you have to. Strangely enough, there are lots of places I'd rather be than with you. Alone, for example."

"You know," he said, as he politely pulled out a chair for her, "I like you like this. I mean, I could if I tried. This is the first time I have ever seen you when you weren't swinging the figurative female lasso round and round."

"Compliments from you are more unpleasant than anything else could be. Light the menu, will you?"

He touched the stud that illuminated the menu screen. She studied it for a moment, and then dialed the code numbers of the items she wanted. Jeremy studied her as she did so.

She was an amazing girl, he admitted grudgingly. How she looked, what she did, what she was—amazing. Her smooth brow was crinkled a bit now, between the eyes.

one of them will end up winning? You as a parent would want to see all of your children doing well. God, as our Father, feels the same way.

When we gamble we are saying to God, "We can't wait for Your blessings to manifest so we will take our chances with satan's worldly games." We then take the seed we received from whatever source of income that God blessed us to have and we use that seed to gamble with. If we win, we thank God that we won, while many others are losers. Your focus is not on the Kingdom of God at all. It is only on you. Because you are just concerned about what you can get no matter who gets hurt. You see, people who gamble are impatient and lack the understanding of God's love. They are allowing greed and selfishness to control them. Now, although you may not care, God does.

You may say, "We do the same thing with stocks." Not true. All who invested in that stock will win or they will all lose. An investment has to do with the perception of the economy doing well. This fits the godly system of the way things should be done. With gambling, statistics have shown that people who have had great winnings experience the curse that comes with gambling, such as losing family and friends. You may say, "Give me the money, I don't need them any way." But, that's not true. People are put in your life for a reason, whether good or bad, and one day you will miss them and perhaps even need them.

The greatest investment you can make is planting seed in the Kingdom of God through winning souls and giving so that the Gospel can be preached all over the world. You can do this by giving your time, tithes and offerings to God. God wants to bless your life. But He needs you to be in position to receive it.

Will a man rob God? Yet ye have robbed me. But ye say, Wherein have ye robbed thee? In tithes and offerings. Ye are cursed with a curse: for ye have robbed me, even this whole nation. Bring ye all the tithes into the storehouse, that there may be meat in mine house and prove me now herewith, saith the Lord of hosts, if I will not open you the windows of heaven, and pour you out a blessing, that there shall not be room enough to receive it. And I will rebuke the devourer for your sakes, and he shall not destroy the fruits of your ground:neither shall your vine cast her fruit before the time in the field, saith the LORD of hosts. And all nations shall call you blessed: for ye shall be a delightsome land, saith the Lord of hosts.

(Malachi 3:8-12)

Drunkards

Some people can come up with all sorts of reasons why it is okay to drink wine or beverages that will cause them to be intoxicated. They will tell you, "Even Jesus drank wine." Did Jesus drink fermented wine? When you read the Word of God, you should try to understand it in the context in which it is speaking, as well as the place and the time. We should understand how words were used in that time period.

When the Bible says Jesus drank wine, does that mean He drank intoxicating wine or was it simply fresh grape juice- wine? Both wine and strong drink exist in the Bible. However, Jesus drank grape juice-wine, which is fresh juice squeezed from grapes. The wine that God approved of is non-alcoholic juice-wine from fruit off of the vine, such as grapes and berries. This is the origin of where we get wine.

There are people who have taken the word, *wine,* that Jesus drank in the Bible, out of context. The words we know today as *grape juice* did not exist in biblical times.

In biblical times, it was all called *wine.* When grapes and berries are squeezed to make juice, it was called *wine.* If grape juice is left alone for a period of time without refrigeration, it begins to ferment and become an intoxicating wine or strong drink. In the Scripture below which tells of Jesus turning the water into wine, the governor said to the bridegroom, "You have saved the best for last." He was referring to the fresh grape juice-wine that Jesus had changed from water into wine.

Fermented wine can be produced quicker by adding chemicals and other things to it. When this it done, the wine then becomes intoxicating, creating a very strong drink. When people drink fermented wine, it affects their behavior. This is different from drinking fresh grape juice-wine. If you drink fresh grape juice and then drink fermented grape juice-wine, you would clearly say that the fresh grape juice- wine tastes better, unless you prefer the content of alcohol over fresh juice.

When the ruler of the feast had tasted the water that was made wine, and knew not whence it was: (but the servants which drew the water knew;) the governor of the feast called the bridegroom, And saith unto him, Every man at the beginning doth set forth good wine; and when men have well drunk, then that which is worse: but thou hast kept the good wine until now.

(John 2:9-10)

Since fermented wine is intoxicating, Jesus did not drink anything that would be harmful to His body. The Bible tells us that Jesus is perfect in every way. He was tried but, He was proven in all points when He was tested. Therefore, if Jesus is perfect, why would we even think He would drink an intoxicating wine when the Word of God teaches men of God not to drink fermented wine or strong drink? God even warned His priests in the Old Testament not to drink strong drink nor wine:

> *And the Lord spake unto Aaron, saying, Do not drink wine nor strong drink, thou, nor thy sons with thee, when ye go into the tabernacle of the congregation, lest ye die: it shall be a statute for ever throughout your generations: And that ye may put difference between holy and unholy, and between unclean and clean.*

> *(Leviticus 10:8-10)*

Since God says, "you are the temple of the Holy Ghost," you should keep your body, which is the temple of God, holy and sanctified before Him. Many people have hurt themselves and others by being drunk or intoxicated.

Why would this be something that God would approve of? He would not. God wants to be with you and in you at all times.

> *Know ye not that ye are the temple of God, and that the Spirit of God dwelleth in you? If any man defile the temple of God, him shall God destroy; for the temple of God is holy, which temple ye are"*

> *(1 Corinthians 3:16-17)*

What? know ye not that your body is the temple of the Holy Ghost which is in you, which ye have of God, and ye are not your own?

(1 Corinthians 6:19)

The word, *wine*, obviously has more than one meaning in the Bible. In fact, where it says Jesus turned the water to wine, this was done in the region of Palestine where it was common to drink grape juice-wine in that time.

The Bible describes when fermented wine or strong drink was used, which was usually when a person was ill and maybe to the point of dying, or when a person was tremendously tormented. So to ease the person from his suffering, he may be given fermented wine or strong drink. In 1 Timothy 5:23, for instance, the Apostle Paul advises Timothy, who was sick, to drink some wine: "Drink no longer water, but use a little wine for thy stomach's sake and thine often infirmities."

People still say today, "You can drink as long as you do it in moderation." Do you *really* know your moderation limit? People don't intend to become drug addicts or alcoholics. It all starts out in moderation. If you are a drinker, you may say, "Well, I have self-control, I drink in moderation. I can quit any time I want." If that's the case, how do you know if you can quit drinking if you never quit? Or do you just stop for a while?

People are influenced by what they see and if you continue to drink, others who follow you or have great admiration for you may copy you. But, what if they don't have self-control? What if they become addicted to drinking or drugs because they imitated you? Remember it started with moderation.

Abstain from all appearance of evil (1 Thessalonians 5:22).

Extortioners

The word *extortion* means *the crime or obtaining money or some other thing of value by the abuse of one's office or authority.*

If you hold an elected office, you have been chosen by the people and placed in this position to help make things better for everyone. People pay taxes so that the towns, cities and states, may be taken care of and the people may be cared for.

To use your position to take advantage of others is wrong. This also goes for church leaders. For instance, if you are a leader in the church and you say to someone, "I will pray for your healing if you pay me this amount," or "If you pay me, I won't tell that you had an abortion," or whatever the case may be, you are committing extortion. If you do this, there is a price to pay for taking advantage of others and it will cost you your place in the Kingdom of God.

People in high-level positions are held to a higher standard. You are not just accountable to the people, but to God.

Covetous

People are covetous when they wrongfully desire what belongs to someone else. When people pursue what belongs to other people they are making a selfish decision to take something from someone without any respect to the other person. They are actually saying: "I want it and I'm going to do whatever I have to, to get it." This is not an attitude of love but an attitude of evil. It is straight from the pit of hell. Satan tried to take what was not his to take and because of his greed, he was kicked out of heaven.

How are thou fallen from heaven, O Lucifer, son of the morning! how art thou cut down to the ground, which didst weaken the nations! For thou hast said in thine heart, I will ascend into heaven, I will exalt my throne above the stars of God: I will sit also upon the mount of the congregation, in the sides of the north: I will ascend above the heights of the clouds; I will be like the most High.

(Isaiah 14:12-14)

We should not violate God's commandment against coveting (Exodus 20:17) by allowing ourselves to be tempted by lustful desires to want someone's husband, wife, children, property, or money. We should not covet what belongs to someone else. Do not let your selfish desires control you; make the decision to rule and reign over your own body.

Hurting others is against the plan of God. The Bible says that God detests those who are covetous and they have no inheritance in God's Kingdom:

For the wicked boastesth of his heart's desire, and blesseth the covetous, whom the Lord abhorreth.

(Psalm 10:3)

For this ye know, that no whoremonger, no unclean person, nor covetous man, who is an idolater, hath any inheritance in the kingdom of Christ and of God.

(Ephesians 5:5)

God's plan for us is that we love one another. If God has given us the authority to fight against principalities, powers, rulers of darkness, then we have the authority to fight against covetousness.

Don't let your flesh control the destination of your soul into eternity. Temptation is always present. Don't let it win. There is no greater blessing than the blessings that God has in store for us. Delight thyself also in the Lord; and he shall give thee the desires of thine heart (Psalm 37:4).

Homosexuality

The last sin that I want to examine in this section and in the next chapter is homosexuality. The sins listed in detail in 1 Corinthians 6:9-10 committed by the unrighteous include those who are effeminate. The word, *effeminate,* refers to those who are homosexual or "abusers of themselves with mankind," (1 Corinthians 6:9). They are also called, *sodomites,* and named after the city of Sodom that God destroyed because of its wickedness.

Clearly, one of the most controversial subjects in the Church and in our society today is homosexuality. Some people would debate whether an alternative lifestyle of homosexuality is actually a sin.

People are unveiling themselves, or as some say, "Coming out of the closet," more than ever in our lifetime and are not ashamed about it. They also are demanding their equal rights. In some instances, gay activists have compared the push for equality for homosexuals in society to the civil rights movement of the 1960s, when black people in this country sought equality.

Gay activists around the country are also pushing for the right to get married to their same-sex partners. Marriage between a man and a woman originated with God and no earthly judge or law can change this. There are blessings and benefits that God has designed for a marriage between a man and a woman.

Now having said this, some people who are gay believe in marriage, but not in the God who created marriage. If that's the case, then why would people want to be in a civil union that comes from the God they don't believe in? Hmm. If you don't believe in God, then what is the benefit of you using God's vows of marriage?

Why should homosexuals, people who choose to live perverted, sinful lifestyles, have special rights? Where do we draw the line? Are we to follow God or man? Accepting homosexuality is the same as saying we should accept rapists, murderers, and drug dealers, and so on. The Bible teaches that a person who commits such sins and does not repent will go to hell for their sin.

My opinion about this doesn't matter; what the Bible says about this is the only thing that matters. If you are offended by what is being said here then, perhaps you might want to consider how you are living. If this is just my opinion, then you had better be absolutely sure that what I'm trying to convey to you is wrong or you won't like where you will be for eternity.

But God shows his anger from heaven against all sinful, wicked people who suppress the truth by their wickedness. They know the truth about God because he has made it obvious to them. Yes, they knew God, but they wouldn't worship him as God or even give him thanks. And they began to think up foolish ideas of what God was like. As a result, their minds became dark and confused. That is why God abandoned them to their shameful desires. Even the women turned against the natural way to have sex and instead indulged in sex with each other. And the men, instead of having normal sexual relations with women, burned with lust for each other. Men did shameful things with other men, and as a result of this sin, they suffered within themselves the penalty they deserved.

—Romans 1:18-19, 26, 27
New Living Translation Version

CHAPTER 5

THE TRUTH ABOUT HOMOSEXUALITY

The lifestyle of homosexuality was once looked upon as shameful. Why isn't this shameful today? Is this because we as believers have gotten away from the things of God? Or are they still shameful today?

The more people in the Church condone what the world does and forget about what the Word of God teaches, the more the world falls into temptation.

As believers, we cannot afford to forget what the Word says. The Bible tells us people are that way because of the lust of the flesh:

> *For all that is in the world, the lust of the flesh, and the lust of the eyes, and the pride of life, is not of the Father, but is of the world.*
>
> *(1 John 2:16)*

God tells us to meditate on His Word both day and night. This would help us to be confident to share God's Word with others as well. People need to know the truth in order to be set free from sin and death.

Men and women of God, you must speak out against wrongdoing; teach the people! For the people who won't step foot into a church to hear the Word of God, I hope this message will reach you.

Homosexuality in the Bible

While we hear a lot about alternative lifestyles today, the fact is homosexuality is not new. It was practiced during Bible times.

Homosexuality had become a major reason why God decided to judge Sodom and Gomorrah, where Lot, Abraham's nephew, lived (Genesis 13:10). The Bible says in Jude 1:7 that the people who lived in Sodom and Gomorrha and the surrounding cities, gave "themselves over to fornication, and going after strange flesh" and ended up "suffering the vengeance of *eternal fire*" (italics added for emphasis).

Because of their sins, God decided to judge the cities. However, Abraham interceded in prayer to God that He might not destroy the cities:

> *And the Lord said, Because the cry of Sodom and Gomorrah is great, and because their sin is very grievous; I will go down now, and see whether they have done altogether according to the cry of it, which is come unto me; and if not, I will know. And the men turned their faces from thence, and went toward*

Sodom: but Abraham stood yet before the Lord. And Abraham drew near, and said, Wilt thou also destroy the righteous with the wicked? Peradventure there be fifty righteous within the city: wilt thou also destroy and not spare the place for the fifty righteous that are therein? That be far from thee to do after this manner, to slay the righteous with the wicked: and that the righteous should be as the wicked, that be far from thee: Shall not the Judge of all the earth do right? And the Lord said, If I find in Sodom fifty righteous within the city, then I will spare all the place for their sakes. And Abraham answered and said, Behold now, I have taken upon me to speak unto the Lord, which am but dust and ashes: Peradventure there shall lack five of the fifty righteous: wilt thou destroy all the city for lack of five? And he said, If I find there forty and five, I will not destroy it. And he spake unto him yet again, and said, Peradventure there shall be forty found there. And he said, I will not do it for forty's sake. And he said unto him, Oh let not the Lord be angry, and I will speak: Peradventure there shall thirty be found there. And he said, I will not do it, if I find thirty there. And he said, Behold now, I have taken upon me to speak unto the Lord: Peradventure there shall be twenty found there. And he said, I will not destroy it for twenty's sake. And he said, Oh let not the Lord be angry, and I will speak yet but this once: Peradventure ten shall be found there. And he said, I will not destroy it for ten's sake. And the Lord went his way, as soon as he had left communing with Abraham: and Abraham returned unto his place.

(Genesis 18:20-33)

Because the Lord could not find ten righteous people in the land, God's judgment would fall on the cities. When God sent his angels to warn Lot of the destruction that was coming, wicked men who saw the angels coming into Lot's house, wanted to have sex with them:

> And there came two angels to Sodom at even; and Lot sat in the gate of Sodom: and Lot seeing them rose up to meet them; and he bowed himself with his face toward the ground; And he said, Behold now, my lords, turn in, I pray you, into your servant's house, and tarry (wait) all night, and wash your feet, and ye shall rise up early, and go on your ways. And they said, Nay; but we will abide in the street all night. And he pressed upon them greatly; and they turned in unto him, and entered into his house; and he made them a feast, and did bake unleavened bread, and they did eat. But before they lay down, the men of the city, even the men of Sodom, compassed the house round, both old and young, all the people from every quarter: And they called unto Lot, and said unto him, Where are the men which came in to thee this night? bring them out unto us, that we may know them
>
> (Genesis 19:1-5)

The word *know* in verse 5 has the same meaning as in the verse in Genesis 4:17, where it talks about Cain having sex with his wife and in Genesis 4:25 where Adam has sex with his wife. The Scripture goes on to say:

> And Lot went out at the door unto them, and shut the door after him, And said, I pray you, brethren, do not so wickedly. Behold now, I have two daughters which have not known man; let me, I pray you, bring them

out unto you, and do ye to them as is good in your eyes: only unto these men do nothing; for therefore came they under the shadow of my roof.

(Genesis 19:6-8)

In verse 8, Lot says his two daughters have not had sex with a man, although the Scripture says in Genesis 19:14 that Lot's two daughters were married. The Adam Clarke Commentary says that Lot had two sons-in-law and it is not stated anywhere else where Lot had more than two daughters. The Scripture says that the sons in law "mocked" Lot because they did not believe what he told them about God's impending destruction. Because of this, they ended up receiving the same judgment as the wicked men who wanted to have sex with the angels who came to Lot's house. The story continues:

And they said (to Lot), Stand back. And they said again, This one fellow came in to sojourn, and he will needs be a judge: now will we deal worse with thee, than with them. And they pressed sore upon the man, even Lot, and came near to break the door. But the men put forth their hand, and pulled Lot into the house to them, and shut to the door. And they smote the men that were at the door of the house with blindness, both small and great: so that they wearied themselves to find the door. And the men said unto Lot, Hast thou here any besides? son in law, and thy sons, and thy daughters, and whatsoever thou hast in the city, bring them out of this place: For we will destroy this place, because the cry of them is waxen great before the face of the Lord; and the Lord hath sent us to destroy it. And Lot went out, and spake unto his sons in law, which married his daughters, and said, Up, get you out of this place; for the Lord will destroy this city. But he seemed as one that mocked unto his sons in law. And when the morning arose, then the angels hastened Lot, saying, Arise, take thy wife, and thy two daughters, which are here; lest thou be consumed in the iniquity of the city. And while he lingered, the men laid hold upon his hand, and upon the hand of his wife, and upon the hand of his two daughters; the Lord being merciful unto him: and they brought him forth, and set him without the city. And it came to pass, when they had brought them forth abroad, that he said, Escape for thy life; look not behind thee, neither stay thou in all the plain; escape to the mountain lest thou be consumed.

(Genesis 19:9-17)

After Lot and his family left the city, God's judgment fell:

Then the Lord rained upon Sodom and upon Gomorrah brimstone and fire from the Lord out of heaven; And he overthrew those cities, and all the plain, and all the inhabitants of the cities, and that which grew upon the ground.

(Genesis 19:24-25)

Just like homosexuality was prevalent in biblical times, the Word of God says that it will continue to happen in the last days in which we are living:

Knowing this first, that there shall come in the last days scoffers, walking after their own lusts.

(2 Peter 3:3)

This know also, that in the last days perilous times shall come. For men shall be lovers of their own selves, covetous, boasters, proud, blasphemers, disobedient to parents, unthankful, unholy, Without natural affection, trucebreakers, false accusers, incontinent, fierce, despisers of those that are good.

(2 Timothy 3:1-3)

Speaking out against homosexuality

People who speak out against homosexuals are now labeled as, "homophobic," because they refuse to accept the homosexual lifestyle. Some even say that homophobics discriminate against gays and lesbians. I see the word, "homophobic," as a label used against people who hate what God hates, which is a perverted lifestyle of sin.

I remember an incident that occurred on Feb. 14, 2007. A former professional basketball player announced that he was gay. One of the sports analysts, who also was a former professional basketball player, was asked during an interview about the announcement. He said that he hated gays. After he said that, the media seemed to take the side of the gay ex- basketball player. The one who said he hated gays was removed from his position as a sports analyst. Nothing was said about the one who openly admitted he was gay. Now I don't believe this statement was a personal attack against the gay individual. I believe the person who made the comment against the gay individual made it because he believes homosexuality is wrong. We should hate evil, not the person but the sin.

Perhaps the forum that he used to express how he felt about homosexuals was wrong. But, if the gay person felt the need to expose his sexual preference to the world then why should we as believers not express our feelings toward this sinful act? We as believers are too quiet about the sins that the world wants to impose on us.

This country was built on godly principles and we should not allow people to change what God has given us as statutes to live by and allow ungodly people to take them away. For instance, prayer was allowed to be taken out of schools years ago. Now, look at our school systems today. We will continue to lose those things that God has set in place if we don't speak up.

If a man had announced that he had raped young women for years, would the media defend him as well? I do not believe the media would do that. So, why then do they defend the homosexuals? Sin is sin. Here was a person saying he hated gays (which is like saying he hates sin and wrongdoing) and defending the sport of basketball, a game he loves, yet he was the one who was criticized by the media! This was a statement against the *sin* of homosexuality that one man was imposing on society to accept.

The sports analyst used the word "hate," which is a strong word for any situation. However, God says He hates sin and homosexuality is sin, *it is not a person*. Sin prevents God's children or His creation from sharing in any part of His Kingdom.

A person who wants to make everyone aware that he or she is gay is trying to receive acceptance from the people who disagree with this lifestyle. Homosexuals want to be accepted in a world that says homosexuality is wrong. The truth of the matter is, it is not acceptable, not because people agree or disagree that it's wrong. It is wrong because God says it is wrong and we are not to call "good," what God says is "evil":

> *Woe unto them that call evil good, and good evil; that put darkness for light, and light for darkness; that put bitter for sweet, and sweet for bitter!*

> *(Isaiah 5:20)*

Ye that love the Lord, hate evil: he preserveth the souls of his saints; he delivereth them out of the hand of the wicked.

(Psalm 97:10)

Whoso rewardeth evil for good, evil shall not depart from his house.

(Proverbs 17:13)

If people who are living the lifestyle of homosexuality feel so comfortable with what they are doing, then why do they feel the need to have people accept them? Because deep down inside of them, they hear a small voice telling them that what they are doing is wrong.

We are taught to love people, but not their wrongdoings. Have we come to the point that we should accept the homosexual lifestyle, even though we know that it is not accepted by God? No, we should not support it in any way or call this evil, good, by accepting it. God forbid!

We have a God-given right to stand for what's right without allowing people to impose a lifestyle of sin on us.

We should pray and share the Word of God about sin and reveal the truth to expose sin. To say that God made people homosexual or gay is an insult to our beliefs and to the Word of God.

What should we do? Continue to love them and share the truth with them.

Being gay: A choice or born that way?

Are some people born gay? NO! Absolutely not. It is impossible. Yes, I said it, IMPOSSIBLE! I know that this has raised doubts even in some Christian believers. Why is this even an issue among people today? *Why are so many people believing that they are born gay and lesbian? This is because so many people are slack concerning the Word of God.* They know the truth, but the Word of God teaches that satan has "blinded them that believe not." Because of their lustful desires, they reject the truth. So, they *choose* sin over God.

Now people may say, "How can you say that? You are not a doctor, Mr. Know-it-all." Well, I can say it based on the truth of the Word of God. A thief is not known as a thief until he or she steals something, a rapist is not a rapist until he or she rapes someone, a murderer is not a murderer until he or she kills someone. Therefore, a homosexual is not a homosexual until he or she has sex with someone of the same sex. This means an action took place. Now, what is in a person's heart is between that person and God and no one can judge the heart but God.

There are men who have feminine traits and there are women who have masculine traits. However, this does not make them homosexuals. It's the actual act of sexual intercourse that makes them homosexual or lesbians.

There are some people who are hermaphrodites, meaning they were born with both male and female sexual organs. How do we respond to the question of "What about people born with both organs? Are they gay?" The answer is: "No."

When I was asked about hermaphrodites, I was not sure how to respond until I read the Word of God and heard a woman who was born with both organs speak about it. She said that only one of the organs is dominant, or works. She also said that she became pregnant after being placed in a men's prison where she was raped.

This shows that a person having both sexual organs has a type of birth defect. Besides that, the person knows whether they are male or female and they don't get to choose which one they want to work. It's not a flip-on switch that allows the person to choose. If the person is a man he knows it and has the ability to plant a seed, and if it is a woman she has the ability to get pregnant, like the woman who I heard speak on the subject.

Some people have made their decision to be gay or lesbian based on different circumstances or on tragic situations that they have gone through. For example, some people choose the gay or lesbian lifestyle because they were either molested or raped or experienced some other form of abuse. The trauma of being abused has affected them in such a way that they no longer want to be the person that they once were before the tragic incident. For the most part, they either want to hurt someone else or they become a person who just doesn't care any more, and some hide it. These are hurting people who are trying to disguise their hurt by hiding inside another character. In reality, these are very confused people.

On the other hand, some have freely chosen to be this way after being influenced by others. Some homosexuals believe, or have at some time believed, in God. But they choose to put God on their level and believe that God will accept them the way they are because He understands their situation. This is really a trick of the devil.

Some may even feel that it's okay to be gay or lesbian because God let something tragic happen to them. No, it is not okay by God. This is far from the truth. Those who believe this way are going by their feelings and are being deceived by satan.

Who we are is not based on the tragedies we go through or on how we feel. Although feelings are important, *we should not allow our feelings to control our actions, especially when they are contrary to the Word of God!* I may feel a certain way, but that does not change the design of who I am inside. You will always be the man or the woman that God made you to be. When an automobile factory builds a car, no matter what you add to it, it is still a car. So that means no matter what you add to a Camaro, or even what you take away from it, it is still what it was designed to be–a Camaro.

You are what God designed you to be–a man or a woman, regardless of what you add, cut, or snip off. Changing your appearance does not change you at all. It only changes the outward appearance. Joe is still Joe and not Josephine. Josephine is still Josephine and not Joe. You can change your body, your name and your complexion, but your soul will remain the same.

Some in the medical profession may argue that people are born gay or lesbian because of something on the left side or right side of their brain. What a mess! Listen people, stop falling for this trick of satan.

Homosexuality is a lifestyle of sin. *Whose report do you believe?* Read your Bible! God doesn't make mistakes. Don't roll the dice on eternity for your life.

You might ask, "Who cares about people's sexual preference?" God does. God loves people. It's the *sins* of the people that God hates. You cannot live a sinful lifestyle and believe that you will go to heaven. You will not, even though the Bible says that it is not God's will that any man perish.

> *The Lord is not slack concerning his promise, as some men count slackness; but is longsuffering to us-ward, not willing that any should perish, but that all should come to repentance.*

> *(2 Peter 3:9)*

All of us will stand in the presence of God one day, including those who live a lifestyle which God calls "an abomination." The word *abomination* means something that is shameful or something that is immoral or disgusting. This goes for women as well.

> *If a man also lie with mankind, as he lieth with a woman, both of them have committed anabomination: they shall surely be put to death; their blood shall be upon them.*

> *(Leviticus 20:13)*

When people participate in wrongdoing, which includes the homosexual lifestyle, unfortunately they will suffer the consequences of their actions. If we live our life without order, then we live it without God. We know that God is a God of order. The Apostle Paul says, "Let all things be done decently and in order," 1 Corinthians 14:40.

God is also a God of judgment. The Bible says judgment will be upon those who reject God's way of living. If you choose disorder, you have chosen to be evil and as Jesus said in John 8:44, you become like your father, the devil:

> *Ye are of your father the devil, and the lusts of your father ye will do. He was a murderer from the beginning, and abode not in the truth, because there is no truth in him. When he speaketh a lie, he speaketh of his own: for he is a liar, and the father of it.*

God encourages us in His Word to choose good and shun evil:

> *Hate the evil, and love the good, and establish judgment in the gate: it may be that the Lord God of hosts will be gracious unto the remnant of Joseph.*
>
> *(Amos 5:15)*

> *Let love be without dissimulation. Abhor that which is evil; cleave to that which is good.*
>
> *(Romans 12:9)*

In other words, *we ought to hate what God hates and love what He loves.* God cannot stop us from choosing a sinful lifestyle, but He will judge us for it. That is why we ought to love people enough to *share the truth about what God says about sin.*

Turning Back to God

As you can see, I felt led to spend more time on the topic of homosexuality because there is so much confusion about this sin today.

God has given me many Scriptures dealing with this subject because it is so important now for people to know the truth about what the Bible says about this sin.

Life here as we know it is not forever. There is nothing to argue or debate. My heart goes out to anyone who, after reading this book, is still confused about what God says about what is sin. This book only touches on the surface of those things that separate us from God. To learn more about what separates us from God, you need to study His Word for yourself.

I am not writing to insult or attack anyone but to help set free those who are lost or confused, or unsure about what sin is, or just don't know what to think of God. I hope and pray that this is helpful to you and that it will encourage you to develop a personal relationship with God.

Everyone has challenges in their life, but faith in God through His Son, Jesus Christ, and the Word of God will sustain you. It is time for you to turn back to God.

> *If my people, which are called by my name, shall humble themselves, and pray, and seek my face, and turn from their wicked ways; then will I hear from heaven, and will forgive their sin, and will heal their land.*

> *(2 Chronicles 7:14)*

EPILOGUE
NOW IS THE TIME
OF SALVATION

If you want to spend eternity with God, you need to make Jesus Christ the Lord over your life. If you have not received Jesus as Lord and you desire to, you can make a confession of faith right now.

Read Romans 10:8-10 and begin to apply the Word of God to your life.

> *But what saith it? The word is nigh thee, even in thy mouth, and in thy heart: that is, the word of faith, which we preach; That if thou shalt confess with thy mouth the Lord Jesus, and shalt believe in thine heart that God hath raised him from the dead, thou shalt be saved. For with the heart man believeth unto righteousness; and with the mouth confession is made unto salvation.*
>
> *(Romans 10:8-10)*

If you commit yourself to the Lord, you will never be the same again. You can't change yourself, only God can change you. Remember, we all need God's help.

If you want to turn your life over to the Lord, then pray this prayer with me:

> *Father God, I come to you for forgiveness, I repent of sin, I choose to turn away from it. I believe that Jesus is the Son of God. I believe Jesus died for me and He is risen and now sitting on the right hand of majesty. I now make Jesus Christ my personal Lord and Savior, and Master of my life. Thank you, Lord, for receiving me as your son/ daughter. I am now born again.*

Rededication

You may say, "I am already saved but I have not been living according to the Word of God." If this is the case, then you can rededicate your life to Christ. Read 1 John 1:9 which says, "If we confess our sins, he is faithful and just to forgive us our sins, and to cleanse us from all unrighteousness." Now, pray this prayer of rededication with me:

> *Father God, forgive me for I have sinned against you. I now confess my sin (whatever your sin may be) and choose to turn away from my wrongdoing and turn back to you, Lord. Your Word says that if I confess my sins, you are faithful and just to forgive me of my sins, and you will cleanse me from all unrighteousness. I thank you Lord for Your forgiveness and for receiving me back as your son/daughter, in Jesus' Name.*

Theodore Sturgeon

She used to look like that in college once in a while. It generally signified that she was out of her depth, and it also meant that she was about to do something about it, like flapping her eyelids at a vulnerable professor, or cribbing from someone else's paper.

Bulldozer Treatment

Frowning, Jeremy studied Phyllis for several minutes more. Then he spoke.

"Tell me something," he said. "Exactly how was this thing supposed to go?"

"I don't know what you mean."

His voice tuned itself to his strained patience. "I mean, what was supposed to happen here? You would meet me at the gate, or you would hunt me up, and then what?"

"You seem to know everything. Answer your own questions."

"All right. You were going to overcome my time-honored distaste of you and give me the business—most likely the remorse angle. The time you pulled that factory-lease out from under us for the benefit of a cosmetic factory—and General Export, who were starting in the pipe business—you are sorry about that. The time Hal fell for Dolly Holleson and you told her so many lies about him that she up and married somebody else—you're sorry about that too. The time you—" His voice got thick—"accepted my ring, all of my grand old 'forgive and forget' attitude, and a third of our company stock, only to turn the stock over to Genex and tell me to go fly it—that was an awful misunderstanding!"

"You know, Phyl, if I had known when I gave you the stock that Hal had phonied up the stock certificate, I'd have killed him, I think. He took the chance. Felt that if you were on the up-and-up he could straighten out the stock later. If you weren't—well, nothing would be lost but a little peace of mind. Mine." He breathed very deeply, once. "Anyhow, Hal thinks you're poison, and I think you're poison, and I don't know what in the universe you think you are, but certainly it isn't anything that will get a new pipe-stowage process out of me."

"You really slug when you start, don't you?" she whispered. He had never seen her eyes so big, nor her face so white. "And you don't mind lowering your sights, to mix a metaphor."

"I adjust to the most obvious target," he said bluntly. "Why don't you get sore? Why don't you leave?"

Slowly, with a small, tragic smile, she rose. "Watch," she said.

9

Memory

She turned toward the door. At a far table, a man rose and sauntered toward the exit. Behind Jeremy, there was a scraping of chairs on the glossy flooring, and the two men who had followed her from the ship went past.

The man at the door, a suave-looking individual, lean and white-templed, folded his arms and leaned against the wall just out of range of the photocell which opened the door. When Phyllis drew abreast he spoke softly to her. She stopped and shook her head. He smiled then, and shook his. She bit her lip, lowered her head a little and moved toward the door again. So smoothly that it did not seem swift at all, he blocked her.

The other two men reached them, greeted her effusively, took an arm each and led her back toward their table, talking and laughing. When they neared Jeremy's place, they released her and went back to their own table, leaving her standing alone, staring at Jeremy with angry and terrified eyes. The whole thing was done so smoothly that no occupant of the restaurant seemed to notice.

"I have just seen something very lovely," said Jeremy happily. "A pushing-around with you involved, where you are getting pushed for a change. Now come and sit down and tell me all about it in a sisterly fashion."

She came. Again he was struck with the difference in her, the air of being out of her depth. She sank into her chair, her eyes averted from his. She put her hands tight together on the table, but they would not stop shaking. She volunteered nothing.

He reached over the centerpiece of the table and opened the cold-chamber on her side, removing the drink she had ordered. Pushing it across to her, he said gently:

"Gulp some of that and for once in your life give me a straight story. Whose side are you on besides your own? How did it happen? And why do these dawn-men take such an interest in leaving you alone, providing it's with me?"

"Everything's gone wrong. You—you know too much, Jeremy. And you don't know enough. All right, I'll tell you. Telling you won't help me—I mean, you won't help me, no matter what. I thought I could get what I wanted out of you without your ever knowing that they—that I—"

"That they have the heat on you," supplemented Jeremy. "Source, Genex. Temperature, high." He shook his head wonderingly. "That's always been the trouble with you, Phyl. So self-sufficient. Never asked anyone for help in your life. There was always a way out, generally paved with somebody's face. I gather that Genex is as wise to you as I am."

Theodore Sturgeon

*

She nodded, with a submissiveness which wrung something within him. His hand went out toward her. He drew it back without touching her.

He said, "Talk, now."

"I was doing all right," she said in a low voice. "I pulled lots of–of deals for General Export. They want everything. They want the entire Colonial trade–ships, supplies, personnel, everything. They're getting it, too, any and every way they can. They'll have Mars when they're through."

"Then what? They're still under government authority."

"Oh, it's long-range, Jeremy. You remember your history. There's a colonial phase, after discovery and exploration. Colonizing is a job in itself–development doesn't really set in for quite a while. Nowadays, of course, the whole process is enormously speeded up. You know the potentialities of Mars. Uranium, iron, diamond-coal and drugs. Why, it's an unlimited opportunity for whoever controls it. For perhaps two generations, Mars will look to Earth for government and guidance. But then there will be patriots, Jeremy. Earth will find herself with a competitor instead of a dominion. And the way that competitor will be run will gradually swing the direction of control the other way–or else. Genex isn't out after a world. Genex wants two worlds–the system–the galaxy, if you like. But it will be for Genex and its heirs; it won't be for the little guy."

Jeremy sat back and stared at her, amazed. "You figured all that out yourself? I can't believe it. No, by heaven, I don't believe it. Whom are you quoting?"

"Hal Jedd," she said with an effort.

"Well, well, well!" He took out Hal's letter and opened it. Her eyes darted to it, to his face, and down again. "Don't play," Jeremy said grimly. "I know you've seen this. You and every stooge Genex could put on it." He glanced through the letter, speared a sentence with his finger, and read aloud: "'Phyllis Exeter due. I got quite chummy with her while she was out here in Thor City.'"

"That's what put me in this spot," she said with sudden bitterness. "Yes, I saw him. Lots. The word got around that he had developed something radical in the line of pipe stowage. He has a suitcase-size lab back of his office, you know. Well, I was put on it."

"You volunteered–isn't that more like it? You said, 'Let me at the sucker. I've been able to wind him and his dopey brother around my finger since we were kids; and besides, I have a little score to settle. They're one up on me.' That right?"

11

Memory

She almost laughed. "I didn't call him a sucker," she said faintly. She took a swallow of her drink. "Take care of the steak, will you, Jeremy? I'm hungry."

Jeremy took the raw steak out of the cold compartment. It was tenderized and seasoned. He slid it into the induction-heater.

"How do you like it?" he asked.

"Seared and rare," she answered.

He adjusted the controls and closed the drawer, while she continued.

"I saw a lot of Hal. He got under my skin, Jeremy. Not anything about him personally—I don't go for his type. These scholarly boys leave me cold. I like big men with blond hair, strong enough to smack a gal down when she deserves it, or even to keep their hands off her. And maybe with a little cleft in a square jaw—"

Unconsciously fingering just such a concavity on his chin, Jeremy threw back his blond head and snapped, "Baloney to you and your shopping lists! Go on with the yarn. What did get under your skin?"

"What he had to say about Genex. I don't know—maybe I never bothered to take it apart before. Maybe my paychecks and bonuses kept me from thinking. Whatever it was that happened, it happened so gradually that I didn't notice it. But the things he said about long-range thinking—well, here I was on the inside and knowing even more about what went with Genex than he did. The more I looked at it, the less I liked it. Maybe I should have left Hal alone. Maybe I should have tuned him out while he talked. But, as I said before, he had me before I knew what was happening."

*

Jeremy smiled. "Hal's like that. He has a theory that a quiet voice in a noisy room is louder than a shout. He thinks quietly and loud that way too." The centerpiece chimed softly and the drawer slid out. Jeremy took the plate-tongs from the rack and lifted the steak and its perfectly cooked side-dishes over to Phyllis.

"Thanks. Well, I met a boy at Fort Wargod. A blue-eyed innocent of a cadet. Maybe it was moonlight. Moonlight's twice as tricky on Mars, you know. Maybe it's because I'm a little crazy, and can't resist trying things out on people. Well, this kid needed to be impressed worse than anyone I ever met. Before I knew it we were on the parapet looking at Earth, hanging out there so bright and blue, and I was spilling all this stuff about colonies, dominions, and the patriotism of the second-generation Martian. Loose talk. Really, I don't know how much of it I believed myself."

Theodore Sturgeon

She shook herself suddenly, all over, as if trying to wriggle out of something tight and hot. Pulling herself together with an effort, she cut into her steak busily.

"Well," she said after she had swallowed the first bite, "my blue-eyed babe in the woods turned out to be a Genex man, put there for the specific purpose of finding out where my indoctrination stood."

Jeremy roared with laughter, a great cruel burst of it. He cut it off instantly and leaned forward. "So it happened to you," he said viciously. "I'm mighty glad to hear it. Some sweet and gentle character made you open up your heart, did he? Tell me something, slicker—did you try to give him some of your company's stock?"

This hit home. In sudden anger she stopped eating and cursed Jeremy. Then all at once, she smiled and shrugged. It was an odd little gesture, and the resignation in it made that something within him flinch again. Phyllis had tried so hard, for so long, to cover up that soft, lost part of her. She had succeeded so well, until now. She was such a magnificent product of her own determinations, and it hurt him to see such a product spoiled, even though he hated everything it represented. So he said, "I'm sorry," and to his surprise, the words tasted good in his mouth.

"So here I am," she said in a low voice. "I failed with Hal, as I should have expected. I got quite a carpeting for it, and for that business with the cadet. And then Hal wrote that letter. Genex carries the mails. Every big brain in the place, and a lot of little ones, has been racking over it ever since. And they put me on to you. This is supposed to be my last chance—my double or nothing play. If I get that process from you, I get back where I was. On probation, of course, but I'll string along with Genex. If I fail, I'm done. Outside of Genex there isn't much doing, and I don't doubt that I'm pretty thoroughly blacklisted."

"You are," he said flatly. "I get the score now. These plugs around here are supposed to keep you with me until you get the info. *Hmm.* Suppose I leave?"

"I go with you. I keep after you, I catch up with you some way, I keep trying."

"How long is this supposed to go on?"

"Until I get the process. Or until Genex gets the pipe hauling contract from the Government. In which case I'm automatically out."

"Suppose you quit trying?"

"Then I'm out, as of that moment."

"In other words, your fate is in my hands, to coin a phrase."

"I guess it is, Jeremy." And to his utter astonishment, she began to cry with her mouth open. For such an accomplished actress, she did it very badly indeed. Her

13

Memory

heart was in it.

Jeremy sat back and watched her, his brain racing. Hal's letter had taken on a few new meanings, but not enough. "Be good, little man." The rest of that old routine was, "And if you can't be good, be careful." Well, maybe he could have been more careful, but Phyllis seemed to have responded well enough to the bulldozer treatment. Jeremy knew what was the matter with her. She was scared. She had lived by her not inconsiderable wits for a long time, and the clear picture of the end of the line she was facing was a frightening one.

But what about the process? Now it was up to Jeremy to figure it out!

Plastic Compact

Hal had done his astute best to explain the process to Jeremy Jedd in that letter. Somewhere in that letter, somewhere in the odd fact of Phyllis's being here—in these three places were components of the process.

She was quieter now.

"Sorry," she sniffled. "I'm in a bad way, I guess. Do you know why I was crying? It was because you didn't get up and leave when I told you all this. You will help me, Jeremy? You will?"

"Help you? How can I?"

"Tell me the process." She leaned closer, excitedly. "Or tell me something almost as good as your process, but better than what Genex has."

"You're very flattering." She really thought he had the process, then. Be good, little man. He'd have to be. But *good*. "I gather Genex has set up a welding plant on Mars. Why are they worried?"

"Power," she answered. "There are only two power-piles on Mars, and they're worked to the limit. They're so heavy, with the shielding and all. Shipping space is so scarce, with foodstuffs, development equipment and so on, that piles aren't set up until they are absolutely essential. Power is rationed, and it is costing Genex a fortune for the piddling amount they need to process sheet-stock into pipe. Their advantage, of course, is to procure the space for themselves and get rid of one more independent outfit."

"Uh-huh. The fight is really over a much bigger thing than pipe. *Hmm*. And the outfit that finds a way to ship pipe in less space than sheet-stock, gets the contract and for once has a solid footing against the corporation's expansion."

"But how can you do it, Jeremy? How can you possibly ship pipe in less space than stacks of plastic sheet?"

He smiled. "You really think I'll tell you, don't you? I have no reason to trust you. You have thrown yourself on my mercy, more or less, and given me the choice of saving your skin—your career, anyway—I suppose you call it that—at the risk of having you hand the process to Genex and not only kill off Jedd and Jedd but also kill the brightest chance in fifty years of checking the monopoly. Nope. I'm telling you nothing." I wish someone would tell me, he added to himself.

"But you still stick around," she said thoughtfully. "You met me at the spaceport, you don't throw me to the wolves when you have a chance, you—why, you don't know the process yourself!"

"On the contrary. I'm just sitting here cruelly amusing myself. I've waited years to see you crawl."

"I'm not going to listen to you," she said tightly. "I think I'm right. The only thing I can do is to help you to figure it out. That letter. You. Me. The process is right here at this table, if we can only find out how to put it together."

"This is going to be very entertaining," said Jeremy, far more jovially than he felt. How could this girl, who in the long run operated so stupidly, be so incredibly sharp in detail? "Where would you start?"

"With the letter," she said promptly. She closed her eyes and her lips moved. It dawned on him that she had thoroughly memorized the letter. She opened her eyes wide and asked, "Who is Budgie?"

"A childhood companion," he said, a little taken aback.

"That's a lie. Every fairly close associate you have ever had in your life has been checked."

Jeremy's mouth slowly opened. Then he brought a hand crashing down on the table and bellowed with laughter.

"Do you mean to tell me," he gasped, "that Genex's investigators have been gravely looking through lists of my schoolmates, cousins, bartenders and dates looking for *Budgie?*"

"We—they tried everything," she said, and added, "Stop that silly cackling. Who was it?"

He held up an irritating forefinger. "Ah-ah! Manners, now. Let us act like ladies and gentlemen, chicken, or I send you to the salt mines."

"I'm sorry," she said angrily. He set his mouth. "I'm sorry," she said with a great deal more sincerity.

Memory

"Better," he said. "Now then, I don't think it'll hurt to tell you. Budgie was a parakeet we used to have. He was around very nearly twenty years. We gave him a fine funeral."

*

The girl stared at him, her eyes glittering with disbelief.

"And yet, according to that letter, the process is nothing Budgie couldn't have told you. Jeremy, I don't believe you. Who was Budgie?"

"So help me, the only Budgie I ever knew was that bird. He swore like a soybean farmer in a urea factory, he did. We called him Budgie because he was a budgerigar, or, to you, a Zebra Parakeet. A budgerigar is the talkingest bird that ever lived."

"What?" she said in disgust. "A creature with memory and no brains could tell you what the process is?" Jeremy started, and she asked, "What's the matter? Have a rush of brains to the head?"

While he fumbled for an answer, she leaned back with narrowed eyes. "I came awfully close to it that time, didn't I? Come clean, Jeremy. You've known about the process ever since you were a kid, now, haven't you?"

"You've got it," he mumbled. She's got it? Who's got what? He clapped his hand to his head. "Memory without brains. That's me."

They stared at each other. "If only I knew a little more about plastics," she breathed. "Or even about your brother. I'll bet if I knew as much about the way Hal's mind works as you do, I could sit right down and write that process out."

Jeremy stared at her and knew she told the truth. His was a quick mind as well as an encyclopedic one, but she was his master at quick intuitive reasoning. A wild plan flitted through his mind—to leap up and rush out, to draw an attack from one of the Genex men who waited patiently for Phyllis to do her work; to prefer charges against the corporation, perhaps. But he rejected it instantly.

They were too clever for that. They would let him go. One of their plastics engineers would work with Phyllis until some hunch she had gotten made sense to him. Then what? Well, either he would figure it out in time or he wouldn't. If not, he was sunk. If so, Genex would so radically underbid his pipe to drive him out that he would be sunk anyway.

"*Hal!*" The name slipped from his lips, so profound was his sudden wish for his brother. Hal could set him straight with a word, if only he could send the word.

"Me too," whispered Phyllis. "If only I could see Hal once, only for a minute, I'll bet I could—" Suddenly she dived into her handbag, clawing out a pot-pourri of feminine conglomerata. "Where is it? Where is—oh—here." She held a rectangular piece of plastic in her hand. It was blue, smooth, heavy.

"What's that?"

"Just a compact. A lighter. A torch. One of those things. But Hal gave it to me. And I'm just mystic enough to think it'll help me think. He had his hands on it. Didn't you know that all women—even modern women—are witches?" She closed her eyes, clutching the compact, frowning in concentration.

Staring at her, Jeremy frowned too, and thought harder than ever in his life before. Something about memory without brains. Something—and then a line in the letter swam before his mind's eye.

I'd like you to meet her when the rocket-ship docks. She really has what it takes.

"Give me that," he spat, and snatched it roughly out of her grasp. Instinctively, she reached for it. He batted her hand out of the way, hard. She sat on the edge of her chair, her nostrils dilated, rubbing her hand and watching him like a cat.

He turned it over and over, shook it, smelled it, felt it. He opened it, shook out the tinted powders, cracked the mirror retainer with his thumb and slid the glass out. There was nothing unusual about the compact. A little expensive, perhaps, but not unique at all. There was no trademark.

"Where did Hal get this?"

"He didn't say. Bought it, perhaps. Maybe he made it. He has a little outfit. Give it back to me!"

"I will not." Jeremy fell to studying it again.

"Jereee," she said sweetly.

*

He looked up. She was her old self. She was erect and beautiful and the color was back in her cheeks. Somewhere in a side corner of his mind, he deeply regretted the fact that he admired her so much. She put out her hand. "Give."

"Nope."

She glanced around. "It's evidence. I've been robbed. The property was forcibly taken from me by that man, officer," she said, mimicking a sweet, wronged young thing. "There we were, sitting peacefully over a drink and a snack, when he went berserk and took it away from me and began tearing it apart." Her face went cold and direct again. "Would you tell the nice policeman exactly *why* you wanted to keep it, Jeremy?"

"Not while Genex and the police get along so nicely," he said grudgingly. "Okay.

Memory

I'm open to compromise. You don't know the significance of this piece of plastic. You just might be wrong. If Genex's plastics division can't find out anything about it, you're away out of luck."

"Oh," she said. She glanced around at the Genex watchdogs and shivered. "What's your proposition?"

"I have to find out something more. Just what, I'm not sure. Now think carefully. Exactly what do you remember Hal's saying about this compact?"

"Why, he never said anything, much. Just some philosophical quip about women, about me and plastics. I don't remember it exactly."

"Try."

"It was—it was something like this." She paused, and he knew she was running over and over it in her mind, poking and prodding at it for hidden meanings. Finally she shrugged, and quoted, "'I like giving you plastics, Phyl. Plastics are an analogical approach to women, and some of 'em come pretty close. Some day maybe we'll all be familiar with a plastic that will react differently under the same stimulus, the way you do. Laughter this time, tears the next, whichever seems to be expected.' I didn't think it was very flattering."

Jeremy stared at her, comprehension sparking, flaming, coruscating in his brain. He said hoarsely:

"Give me the compact. I've got to get it to a lab."

"No," she said firmly. She took it out of his unwilling hands. "Frankly, I don't know what you've figured out. But I will, if I kick it around long enough. If I can't, I know those who can. Well," she purred, arching her body, "I'd better run along, Jerry darling. Thank you so much for everything."

The hand that closed on her wrist seemed to be made of beryl steel. "Don't you move," Jeremy said. He said it in a way which kept her from moving. "You can't take that chance. You don't know enough. If you take that away, I'll never know either, and I'd see both of us dead first. I'll make a bargain. Once more. I must make a test on that compact. I can do it right here. Let me do it. You can watch. Whatever happens, your description will be enough for a plastics engineer. It will give us both a break. And if there really is a secret there, you'll have a chance of getting what you want. You'll *know*. You don't know now—you only guess."

It was a long time before she nodded her head.

When she did, he took the compact and, with his knife, scraped off a shaving and dropped it into the ash tray. He took a plate-handler from the warm rack and touched the shaving. Then he put his cigarette to it. Then he held it with the plate-handler and held it in the flame of his cigarette lighter. Part of it burned. He sniffed the smoke, nodded, and set the temperature regulator on the induction-heater.

He dropped the compact in and closed the drawer.

"No!" she shouted. "You're burning it! You've got the process, and you're destroying it so I won't have a chance!" She lunged for the drawer. He caught her wrists, transferred them both to one of his powerful hands, and shook his head.

"Sit tight," he snapped.

*

The centerpiece chimed, and the drawer popped open. Their heads cracked together painfully as they bent to look inside. Neither noticed the pain.

In the bottom of the pan lay a twisted piece of blue plastic. It spread almost all the way across the roomy drawer. It was flat, and followed a series of regular convolutions. It dawned on both of them at the same moment what it was.

Script.

As if the plastic itself were the track of a writing-brush, it spelled the two words:

I REMEMBER

"That's for me," breathed Phyllis. "And I'm a dope. The memory without brains—even I know about that phenomenon. Now that I see it done, I remember a demonstration in school, where a cube was compression-molded into a spool-shape. When it was heated again, it slumped together and formed the original cube. A little sloppy, but a cube nevertheless. With a little refinement, I don't see why extruded pipe shouldn't be compression-molded into rods, bricks, or book-ends and still come out pipe when it's heated. Beats sheet-stock welding a mile. Jeremy, my boy, you may have my melted-up old compact with my blessings. You may frame it and hang it over your lab bench when you come to work for Genex, as you must or starve. 'I remember.' I like that."

"You don't remember how badly you needed help, Phyllis," he said hoarsely. "My help."

"Plastics and women, my boy. Remember?" She rose like a queen, gathered up her belongings and drifted doorward, beckoning imperiously to the watchdogs. Ignoring Jeremy Jedd completely, they followed her out.

Memory

Surprise for Genex

Abruptly Jeremy came to his senses with an inarticulate, animal noise and raced to the door. The lithe man with white hair at his temples stepped in front of him.

"Want something, chum?" he asked softly.

Jeremy raised a hand to sweep the man aside but his eye fell on what the man was holding in his hand. It was a rectangular leatherette needle case. Jeremy had seen them before. A touch of the case, a little pressure on a stud, and you were needled. And the variety of hypos used was peculiarly horrible.

They stood there, frozen, for a long instant. Then someone passed.

A spaceport guard.

"Guard!" Jeremy rapped, leaping backward. "This man's threatening me. Needle!"

The guard bobbled a remarkable Adam's apple at them and then strode toward the white-templed man.

"Give it here, bud."

The man smiled, raised the case, snapped it open and extracted a cigarette. "A joke, guard. Perfectly harmless."

"Ha-ha!" said the guard with his mouth only. He clicked his lips shut and looked at Jeremy with one eyebrow raised. "You sure are jumpy, Blondy," he remarked, and strode off.

Jeremy controlled himself with a prodigious effort and swung on the older man. "Listen, you—"

The man blew smoke at Jeremy. "Better cool down, son," he said kindly. "We joke often, but not always. *Hold it!*" he snapped, watching Jeremy's darkening face. "You can butter me up and down these walls, but I'm only one of a couple of thousand that you'd have to whip afterward. Better go on back now and have another drink." And before Jeremy could move so much as a lip, the man was striding up the corridor in that way which did not seem to be swift.

Balked, frustrated, furious, Jeremy stood for a while and then turned back into the restaurant. He slouched back to his table, kicked the chair out and dropped into it. He could use that plastic-memory stunt to stow pipe. Sure. And when he thought of the low bid that Genex would put up against him, his stomach turned over.

He glowered into the heater drawer, where the blue plastic script told him placidly what he would never forget:

I REMEMBER

And then he thought of Hal's words to Phyllis.

20

Theodore Sturgeon

*

The demonstrations supporting registered bids were made in a public hearing, in the vast offices of the Shipping Space Priority Board. The Space Commissioner, an oldster with a snowy lion's mane and the eyes of an eight-year-old child, had his wattles in his palms and his elbows on his desk. He was flanked by the featureless protocolloids of his well-peopled bureau.

In the wide area before him were three groups of people, each hovering over a tangle of apparatus. Behind them were the rows of seats for the interested public, one third of the seats occupied. The second demonstration was in progress. The first demonstrator and his helpers were dismantling their bulky machine—part brake, part automatic welder, it had produced several hundred feet of inch-and-a-half pipe out of a long and compact bale of sheet-stock.

The galleries had regarded the performance as quite impressive, whether or not they knew that Winfield and Shock, who presented the process, was a General Export affiliate, brought in to establish a figment of competition.

General Export's management had shrewdly chosen a presentable demonstration by a more than presentable demonstrator. She was slender, poised, clear-eyed, clear-voiced, and her hair was green. She was saying:

"—and in spite of the question of simultaneous patent application, General Export will offer this pipe at a lower price per unit shipped than any competitor could conceivably meet, due to a secret treatment of the original plastic."

"Due to the secret mistreatment of competition," growled a man in the gallery, who had once owned a space-line.

*

The demonstrator walked gracefully to a stack of long, slender plastic rods beside her machine and lifted one. "Mr. Commissioner, this rod is twelve feet long and one sixteenth of an inch square. As you will observe, the rod is extremely flexible. Stowage of these rods will therefore be compact and economical, since rectangular holds are not necessary. Bundles of these rods will follow the curves, if any, of the retaining bulkheads, and therefore use every cubic inch of space economically. I shall now demonstrate the creation of usable seamless pipe from these rods."

She stepped over to her machine, slid the rod in at one end, and threw a lever. "This is a very simple heater. On Earth or Mars, particularly on Mars, it may be adequately operated by sun-mirrors, thereby tapping no local power-source."

There was a faint hiss. A small motor whined, and a twelve-foot length of pipe shot out with a dry clatter. She repeated the performance twice more and then bowed respectfully to the Commissioner, who said:

"Thank you very much, Miss Exeter. Next!"

A clerk sang, "Mr. Jeremy Jedd, of Jedd and Jedd! Process, pipe stowage, interplanetary!"

Jeremy stood up, ran off the customary courtesies of the applicant, and then said:

"I am deeply grateful to Miss Exeter for many things. One of these is her concise and well-presented description of the advantages of General Export's plastic-memory process. She has saved me much explanation, for my process is precisely the same. The difference lies in the plastic treatment before and after the processing you see here. I will say at the start that as regards price of the rods I am demonstrating, they cost at least five times as much as those shown by Miss Exeter. I am, apparently, drastically underbid."

Jeremy had to pause then to duck under the wave of comment that swept over the huge room. The Commissioner cleared his throat and raised a forefinger without moving his hand from his chin. A clerk raised a gavel without moving anything but his arm, and brought it down with a crash.

"Get on with it," growled the Commissioner. His tone said, If you can't compete with the other bids, you idiot, why waste my time, or even that of these thousand-odd other people?

Jeremy stepped to his machine, which was almost a duplicate of the one Phyllis Exeter had used, and lifted an end of one of his rods. He did not attempt to lift it all at once; apparently it was quite heavy.

What followed was the same as the previous showing, with one noticeable exception; the pipe came out in a twenty-foot length. Again the room buzzed. This time Jeremy held up his hand. "The greater length of the pipe is an advantage over these other methods, but not the greatest," he said calmly. He threw the heater-control over again—

Without loading in another rod!

A twenty-foot length of pipe joined its predecessor.

Again he pulled the control, and again. Each time a twenty-foot pipe was produced, until six of them lay side by side on the floor. The air above them shimmered very slightly. They were uniform and perfect.

"Mr. Commissioner, I ask that space for shipment of pipe to Mars be allotted to my company because the stowage is as compact as any product on the market,

Theodore Sturgeon

because I can ship approximately nine point three times as much pipe per cube unit as my nearest competitor, and because I can deliver pipe per unit length at eleven per cent cheaper than anyone else on earth! And that in spite of the apparently prohibitively low bid of Miss Exeter's most altruistic firm. Thank you, gentlemen."

"Just a minute, young man!" said the Commissioner. "You have a most remarkable process. I—ah—hear comments to the effect that the pipe was concealed in the machine. Can you give some layman's explanation of this extraordinary effect?"

*

Jeremy smiled as he glanced at the machine in front of him.

"Certainly, sir. My company, you may remember, secured a portion of the space allotted to pipe shipments during your last session, by devising the present method of nesting the smaller diameters of pipe inside the larger ones—a method which was not patentable, which my competitors were slow to discover, but quick to copy.

"In the present case, I very much fear that they have repeated their lack of—if I may say it—logical thoroughness. You see, my pipe is still nested, one inside the other, six taking the space of one, and the whole compressed into the rods you see here."

"You nest pipe of the same diameter?" said the Commissioner incredulously; and that odd, mad, detached part of Jeremy's mind noticed hilariously that the oldster's bright eyes blinked with repressed anger.

"Yes sir, I do, in effect. But it is a question of density. The inner pipe is a condensed plastic—a patented process, by the way. This plastic, while undergoing the 'memorizing' phenomenon so beautifully explained by Miss Exeter, restores its original density as well as its original form. The inner pipe, then, is simply condensed more than the one which surrounds it, and so on until the six are nested. Then the whole is compression, molded into rods of precisely the dimensions of those admirably compact ones produced by General Export.

"Now, when heat treated, the outer pipe returns to its original form and is automatically ejected from the machine. It has, of course, pre-heated the next pipe, which pre-heats the one after. It takes, actually, far less heat per unit length to restore my pipe than it does to restore the pipe of—ah—any of my competitors. A small advantage, however, and merely hair-splitting under the circumstances."

"I feel you deserve many congratulations, Mr. Jedd. Purely as a matter of personal interest, might I ask how you came to discover such a remarkable effect?"

Memory

"Indeed you may, Mr. Commissioner. The process was developed by my brother on Mars. He enlisted the courtesy and kindness of a messenger to send me a sample. It was in the form of a compact—a lady's compact—and when heat treated it separated into a plastic sheet which formed in script the words 'I remember.'"

Jeremy grinned broadly. "It was some time before I realized that there was anything more to be learned from the sample, for the words covered the rest of it. When I put this—this message into my pocket, I saw the rest of the plastic and, guided by a hint in a rather cryptic verbal message concerning women and plastics, I again treated the sample. I got more script. It read, 'Density Two.' Then I knew what he was driving at. I treated it again and got 'Density Three' and still again and got"—he smiled—"a length of pipe. After that it was little trouble for me to analyze the plastic and develop the condensing treatment—I beg your pardon. I think somebody had better get Miss Exeter a glass of water . . . ."

They met that evening, and perhaps it was by accident. She was standing in the shadow near his apartment building when he came home from the lab.

"Jerry?"

"Phyllis! I—I'm sorry."

"Sorry? That's what you say when you realize you did a wrong. I don't think you mean that. Isn't it more a kind of—pity?"

He did not deny it. He said, "What can I do for you?"

"I—I need a job now."

He took her hand and drew her into the pale light. Her hand lay in his like something asleep. "I couldn't give you a job, Phyl."

"Yes, I know, I know. I have never been—faithful. Jerry, I haven't been faithful to myself."

"I don't understand. You've always—"

"Always thought I could take 'em or leave 'em alone. Not so, Jeremy."

"Oh," he said. "Oh, that." He squeezed her hand a little. "Your hands are soft. Maybe that's part of the trouble, Phyl."

"I think I know what you mean. There are jobs for me, but—"

"—not jobs for your wit or your wits."

"I see. I think I can—get there, Jerry."

"I know you can. Good-by, Phyllis."

"Good-by, Jeremy."

There is one job which centuries of human progress has not done away with. No

Theodore Sturgeon

one has developed a self-washing window. When one of mankind's monuments to himself reaches a thousand feet into the air, and its windows must be washed, that washing is a job for a rare type of human. He must be strong, steady, and brave. He must live, away from his job, in ways which do not unfit him for it.

Jeremy was glad when he heard Phyllis was doing this work. He knew then what he had always guessed—that some day she would "get there." He knew it in his heart.